Snow's Meltdown

COFFEE

LOVE

African American Fiction

By Marita Kinney

ISBN- 978-1-953760-21-0

Published by Pure Thoughts Publishing, LLC2055 Gees Mill Rd #316 | Conyers, GA 30013 USA 470-440-0875 | www.purethoughtspublishing.com

Printed in the United States of America

Coffee Love　　　　　　*Marita Kinney*

Snow's Meltdown

COFFEE

LOVE

African American Fiction

By Marita Kinney

Coffee Love   *Marita Kinney*

Introduction

I love my husband. We're practically the perfect couple. I see how people admire us all the time but they have no idea how hard it is to have a good marriage. I mean, I've always wanted to be happy. I wanted to be loved and I was going to make this marriage work no matter what. I wasn't going to give up. I've done that in the past. This is actually my third marriage, but I've grown, I've matured, I've learned and not only that, I'm a believer now. I have the strength that it takes to make my marriage work.

See, when my husband married me, I was a widow. Yeah, I know. I was 26 years old, a widow and prior to becoming a widow, I was divorced. I got married at a very, very early age the first time, had a kid.

Coffee Love   *Marita Kinney*

You know the story. Trying to make things right,
but it didn't work out. I later re-married, had another
kid. Well, and life would have it, he died of cancer.
So, I didn't have too much faith in love until God
softened my heart and allowed me to fall in love
with Mr. Calvin. I call him Mr. Calvin because he's
so prestigious. He looks like a college professor. It
just looks as if his name should have "mister" in
front of it.

But yeah. When I saw him, it was love at first sight.
I had never in my life felt the energy and the
chemistry that was so amazing like when I first met
him. He is truly my coffee love.

Now, I know when you think of coffee, you think of
just a regular, morning beverage that you may have
occasionally or every morning, but coffee means so

much more to me. Coffee saved my marriage. You'll see exactly what I mean. I had no idea how staying consistent with something that you have in common with someone, can always keep you connected.

My name is Savannah and I pray that you can find coffee love in your own life.

Chapter 1
New Home, New Life, New Family

Calvin smiled as he reached in his pocket and pulled out the house key. He quickly gave it to Savannah. "What's this, Calvin?"

"Baby, I want you to be the first to open up the door to our brand-new home."

"Aww. Honey, you're so sweet. Oh my God, this is such a blessing for our family. Ahhhh," Savannah exhaled as she grabbed the key from Calvin and slowly put it into the door and unlocked their beautiful home.

She walked into the house and thanked God as she

heard her voice echo throughout their new home. The kids were so anxious to see their new rooms. "Hey you guys! Slow down, slow down! Luke, Isaac, and Lacey! Stop running now!"

"We will! We will! We just want to see our new room!"

This was the first time the family had been in the home since they first seen it with the realtor over two months ago. "Honey, let them go ahead and find their room. Let's take a look at the house again." Calvin grabbed Savannah's hand and they walked throughout the house smiling proudly. Their marriage was making a lot of progress and they were already fulfilling their dreams together. Calvin looked over at Savannah as she smiled from ear to ear, thanking God and proud of him for taking care of her. She turned and looked Calvin in the eyes. "Baby, you have no idea how much this means to me."

"Well, I hope it means a lot considering how much I paid for the house. You better not leave me after this."

"Shut up. Nobody's going to leave you. You're so silly. I mean, this is a new beginning. I've been through so much and the life that we have right now sometimes seems so far-fetched, now it's reality. I got my man. I have my beautiful children. Not to mention God blessed me with a daughter too. I mean, Lacey's like my baby that I didn't have labor pain with. "They both laughed. " You and Lacey came into my life and added so much more value. I love Lacey and I love you and everything that this

12

new home represents. It represents a new beginning for us."

"I know, baby," Calvin replied. "I feel the same way about you and the boys and I just wanted to provide you with the best possible life that I could. You didn't marry a little boy. You married a grown man and I'm going to take care of this family." They both leaned in and began to passionately kiss.

"Ewwww," the kids said as they walked closer towards the couple. Savannah grabbed her hand and began to wipe off her mouth.

"Oh, sorry guys. We didn't know you were standing there. Do you like your room? Did you guys pick which one you wanted?"

"Yes, ma'am," they all replied.

Calvin couldn't wait to go see the garage. For some reason he loved the garage. Maybe it's because he's good with his hands and he planned to do a lot of projects.

"Well, you guys go ahead and walk around the house together and we'll go check out the garage and see how much space I have. Honey, you know I want to get that motorcycle."

"Oh, trust me. How could I ever forget? That's all you've been talking about. Is the garage big enough for your motorcycle that you don't even have yet?"

Calvin laughed as he walked away. Savannah stared at him the whole entire time, admiring his bow legs and his swag as he continued to walk through the kitchen towards the other end of the house where the garage was located. "Sooo Laccy, can you see us planting flowers outside? We could probably get a pool one day too. We're going to have so much fun in this house."

"I know, I know, I know," the she replied with anticipation.

"Kids, I want you to know how blessed you are." Luke and Isaac smiled from ear to ear. Lacey smiled also, but feeling a bit left out. Savannah noticed her gesture and walked closer to her to give her a hug. "Lacey, I know that you're not going to be here every day with us, but this is just as much your home as it is ours. We're going to decorate your room really pretty and every time you come to stay, this is your house, this is your room. We're going to have everything for you just like you have at your mommy's house. This is always your home too, okay?"

Lacey smiled as she felt better being reassured by Savannah that this was also her home.

Chapter 2
Real Life

"Calvin, did you get the mail today?"

"Yes, I got the mail. I put it right there on the counter. You don't see it?"

"Oh, somebody must have moved it. I have to pay these bills and I can't find the electric bill or anything. I don't know where it is. I know it's due because we've been here for what? Over a month now and I haven't seen the electric bill. The last thing I want to do is have it cut off because I can't pay it."

"Honey, just calm down. It's around here somewhere."

"Okay well, when you find it can you just give it to me so I can make sure that it's paid?"

"Sure, of course. Honey, you know, things are going to be okay. I know moving into this house took a lot more money and I'm spending a lot more money in gas. But it's because we live so far away from our jobs now, but things are going to work out. Why are you so stressed out? Don't you have faith?"

"Calvin, of course I have faith. I'm just saying, you know ... It's not the electric bill that's bothering me."

"Okay. Well, what's up? What's going on? What's bothering you?"

"Last night, your phone rung off the chain. I know it was Lacey's mom. It had to be, but I can't imagine what she would want at that time of night. Lacey is seven years old. She's not an infant. Whatever she needed could have waited. Why does she feel so comfortable calling you all hours of the night?"

"Well, yeah, it was Lacey's mom. She said that Lacey left her book bag over here and she needed it for school."

"Okay. And so, she kept calling all hours of the night expecting you to do what? Take her the book bag?"

"Savannah look, I know this isn't easy for you but you know, it's important that Lacey has what she needs for school. No, I wasn't going to leave in the middle of the night to take her the book bag. Are you silly? I was going to make arrangements to meet her at some point in time today to make sure that Lacey had everything she needed."

"That's what I mean. You guys are always leaving me out of the loop. I'm going that way anyway. I could take Lacey her book bag."

"Do you have an issue with Lacey leaving her book bag or do you have an issue with me seeing her mom?"

"I have an issue with both. When Lacey's here she needs to be responsible and make sure that she has everything she needs when she leaves. Her stuff needs to be packed and ready to go because it causes confusion. That gives her mom just one more reason to call you constantly."

"Baby, it's not like she just calling just to be calling me."

"Oh yeah? And you think I'm Boo Boo the Fool? That woman looks for any excuse possible to call you. I mean, Lacey can stub her toe and she'll call you. Lacey can lose a barrette and she'll call you. You know I just ... I don't understand. I mean, why is she so obsessed with you? You guys have been over for what...seven or eight years? Ya'll broke up when Lacey was how old? Oh, I forgot you two were never together, she's a THOT. She just needs to accept that you have moved on and stop looking for reasons to talk to you. You haven't realized that she'll talk to you anyway she can, even if it means you guys are arguing? Now that she knows that you're Lacey's father, she's trying to punish you. It's not your fault that you have not been there for her."

"You know I do not like arguing with that woman. I just want a relationship with my daughter."

"It's not about you. It's about her. At least you're talking to her. That's why she makes up all these fake arguments, just so she could talk to you."

"All right Savannah. Now, that's enough. You sound really insecure right now."

"Insecure? Insecure? No, I just have a problem with Lacey's mom calling you every hour. I mean, what is there for her to talk about?"

"Lacey's mom has a name."

"So now you're being defensive over Kim?"

"It kills you to say her name, doesn't it?" Calvin started laughing.

"What's so funny?"

"The way you say her name. It's just… you have so much anger and resentment towards her. Baby, you really need to let it go."

"Look, I don't want her interrupting our day."

"So, before you go to work, would you like me to make you a cup of coffee?" Calvin said hoping to calm her down.

"I would like a cup of coffee, but I'm going to be late. I was trying to pay these bills before I got on the road. Like I said, I could've taken Lacey's book bag to her on my lunch break. Um, if you want to go ahead and take it, that's fine. Um, but the offer's out there. I don't mind helping with that."

"Honey, you can take Lacey her book bag. You can take it to her school and drop it off. That's fine. I don't have a problem with that."

"Okay, okay, okay, great. Well, I'll do that because there's no sense in you going all out your way when I'm on that side of town anyway. So, you know, if you find the light bill before you go to work, just text me how much it is so I can go ahead and pay that or you can pay it. It doesn't matter. It just needs to be paid; I know. And yes, I would like a cup of coffee. Did I already tell you that?" Savannah laughed at how foolish she was being. She could no longer remain upset.

Calvin hated to see Savannah so stressed out, but he continued to go ahead and make her coffee as he normally would in the mornings. He understood that having Lacey was difficult because it was true, Kim did find every excuse possible to call him. He didn't know how to diffuse the situation without causing a bigger scene, but he knew that it was time to have a talk with Kim to make her realize that her aggravating phone calls were inappropriate and it was starting to cause confusion in his home and the last thing he wanted to do was to upset Savannah because Kim was being petty and overbearing.

Chapter 3
Coffee

"Lord, I lift your name on high. Lord, I love to sing your praises. I'm so glad you're in my life," Savannah sang as she got dressed for church. Knowing that they were going to be late, she's singing to remain calm. The kids always seemed to take up so much of her morning and of course, Calvin did too, because he loved making love on Sundays before they went to church.

"Hey Savannah. I'm down here making coffee."

"Okay, honey. I'll be down there in just a moment. Tell the kids to sit down. I don't want them to mess up their clothes."

"Okay. Kids, your mom said to sit down and wait for her. She'll be down in just a minute," Calvin repeated. Lacey hated the idea of having two moms and rolled her eyes.

Savannah looked in the mirror as she began to put on her makeup. Life was stressful but Sundays always gave her a relief. She looked forward to going to morning worship. She looked forward to hearing the word of God for inspiration, for motivation and encouragement. She also looked forward to things getting better in her marriage. The marriage was stressful, yes, but Savannah was determined to do everything she was supposed to do as a wife, but the one thing she needed to work on was maintaining her peace and practicing more patience. See, patience was something that she'd always struggled with. Whenever things made her feel uncomfortable, she was ready to give up. She was ready to run, but she was determined to have a successful marriage, even if it meant her changing who she was used to being.

The former First Lady at the church had taught her a lot. She was mentoring her before she died of Cancer. Lady Rose was so graceful, so proud of her husband, happen to also be Calvin's mother. Savannah had always looked up to her for years and asked Lady Rose to be her mentor when she used to work for her. They had their own bond outside of the *Snow Men*. Things seemed to be working out okay between she and Calvin, but Lady Rose had a lot more experience than she. Savannah was certain that things would slowly change as she learned how to become a good wife. She continued to stare at herself in the mirror as she put on her eyeliner, thinking about all the mistakes that she made and being so hard on Calvin when it came to Lacey's mom. She knew that jealousy was going to just push him away and insecurities weren't going to help either. So, she needed to build up her confidence in order to become the wife that she needed to be for him. He was a strong man and he deserved to have a strong woman next to him. "Okay girl, get yourself together," Savannah said as she gave herself a pep talk before, she went downstairs to join her family. She couldn't help but notice the tears that were starting to fill her eyes, realizing she had been through a lot and if she didn't change her ways, she was going to throw everything down the drain. She took a deep breath as she grabbed her purse and walked downstairs to be with her family.

As she stepped onto the landing, she saw Calvin at

the end of the steps waiting for her with a cup of coffee. She couldn't help but smile, because he was so giving. It was as if she was his queen and he just wanted to make her happy. Savannah grabbed the cup of coffee from him and gave him a passionate kiss. She looked at him and said, "Baby, I love you."

Calvin said, "I love you too," with an instant reply. Savannah gazed at his eyes a few second longer, letting him know that she wasn't just saying that she loved him as some sort of cliché, but she really meant it. As they walked out of the house, Savannah was still drinking her hot cup of coffee, sipping it, trying not to spill any on her dress as she walked to the car. She then grabbed the car door. Calvin instantly got upset. "Savannah, what are you doing?" She forgot. Calvin always opened doors for

her, but there was still some independence in her
that was so used to opening her own door. "Baby,
you're going to have to get used to me opening
doors for you. As long as you're with me, you'll
never have to open another door." Savannah smiled
as she got into the car.

Chapter 4
She Still Loves Him

It was Friday night and Calvin and Savannah were looking forward to Lacey coming to visit for the weekend. As always, she was being dropped off by her mother, Kim. Kim loved dropping Lacey off. She just wanted to be nosey. She wanted to see where Lacey was going to be, where Calvin and Savannah were living, what they were driving. She always wanted to be in their business, so dropping Lacey off would give her the opportunity to snoop and to pry. Savannah hated the fact that Lacey was always being dropped off and insisted of meeting at a neutral location somewhere, but Calvin said that things were easier the way they had always been.

As always, Savannah backed off and tried to stay

out of their arrangements. The doorbell rung and
Luke and Lacey ran to the door, excited to see their
sister, Lacey. It had been over a week since they'd
last seen her.

"Boys, stop running towards the door! Get
somewhere and sit down," Savannah instructed
because she wanted to open up the door before
Calvin got a chance to. She definitely did not want
Luke and Isaac to be anywhere near the door
because she never knew how the conversation with
Kim was going to go.

Calvin knew that Savannah wanted to open the
door, so he allowed her to get to the door before he
did. The door opened. You could tell that Kim was
surprised to see Savannah as she had hoped that
Calvin would open the door instead. She stood there

with her cleavage popping out of her dress, wearing a fitted maxi low-cut summer dress and it wasn't even summer. She knew that Kim had done it intentionally, hoping that Calvin would take a glimpse of her double Ds.

"Good morning, Lacey," Savannah addressed Lacey as she hugged her waist, excited to be back home with them. Kim was frustrated. "And hello to you, Kim," Savannah said, Kim not said anything.

"Is Calvin here? I really need to speak to him about something," Kim replied with an attitude.

"Well, yes, he's here. One moment. Calvin," Savannah yelled into the house. "Kim would like to speak with you."

Coffee Love   *Marita Kinney*

"All right. Here I come," Calvin yelled throughout the house. He walked up to the door and he saw Kim standing there as suddenly a smile appeared on her face. "Yeah, what would you like to speak to me about?"

Kim insisted, "I would actually like to speak to you alone."

"Alone? For what? Anything you need to talk to me about, my wife can hear also."

Kim rolled her eyes with disappointment as she hoped to have a private conversation, realizing that Calvin was suddenly drawing the line in the sand, setting boundaries with her that he had never set before. Savannah was proud of him and continued to stand by his side at the door, awaiting what

35

conversation Kim desperately needed to have this morning. "I was just going to say that, um, instead of Lacey packing a bag, I think she needs to keep her stuff at my house and whatever you buy her, she keeps here. That way, she's not forgetting to bring the stuff back home. How does that sound?"

Savannah could read in between the lines and knew that Kim was upset because she dropped Lacey's book bag off to her at school. See, she didn't like the fact that Lacey had a stepmother and going up to her school was a big violation in her eyes. She wanted to keep Savannah completely out of Lacey's life and she didn't want to give her an excuse to go up to her school again. Calvin sighed, "Okay. That's fine with me, but I don't understand why she has to have two sets of everything. The stuff belongs to Lacey and if she wants to take anything from our house home with her, she's welcome to and I'm assuming that while she's at your house, if she wants to bring something with her, it should be okay. I don't understand what the problem is."

Kim replied hesitantly, "The problem is I'm tired of her always leaving stuff and then we have to make arrangements how to get her stuff back. When I send her with things, I'm expecting for her to come home with those same things."

Savannah could tell that there was an argument about to start and she just replied on Calvin's behalf, "Okay, okay, yeah. We understand. That's perfectly fine. We'll make sure that what we have here will stay here and what you have at your house will stay there. Problem solved. No problem. Anything else?" Savannah added.

"No, that's it," said Kim with an attitude. "So, in case you're wondering, Lacey does not have a bag with her. FYI." Calvin laughed sarcastically.

"That's fine sweetie. We have plenty of things here for her to wear," Savannah replied, letting Kim know that they were not worried and already had everything for Lacey at their house. Kim turned away and walked towards her car as Savannah looked up at Calvin and Calvin was disappointed because he always tried to eliminate any drama from Kim whatsoever. As Savannah shut the door, she looked at Calvin and said, "I'm tired of this crap. I'm tired."

"Can we go upstairs and talk about this?" Calvin asked, trying to keep the peace.

"No. Let's talk about this now. The kids are upstairs playing and I just don't know how to deal with all this drama."

"Savannah, you act like I enjoy the drama with Kim. Listen, if you hadn't opened the door, you wouldn't have to have dealt with it, but you put yourself in this drama."

"Excuse me? What do you mean I put myself in this drama?"

"You put yourself in it. It's like you want to be involved. You want to irritate her."

"Yes. You know why? Because she still loves you. I can tell by the way that she looked at you. Don't you see how she comes over here? The type of clothes that she wears?"

"I don't ... Listen, I don't pay attention to her and I'm tired of you always mentioning all my baby mama drama. I mean, if your son's father was in his life, you'd probably have drama too."

"What do you mean if he was in his life?"

"Savannah, one of the fathers is nowhere to be found and the other one is deceased. That's why you don't have drama, so stop trying to judge me."

"Judge you? That's what you think? You think I'm judging you? I'm not judging you. I'm just tired of you allowing her to dictate everything that's happening and you act like it's my fault that Luke's dad isn't in the picture. I can't make him be a father to him and Isaac's father is deceased. I can't help it that he's dead. Neither can he. Why are you throwing that up in my face as if it's my fault they're not around? I can't help that."

Calvin looked at her in anger. "You don't want me to be involved with my daughter. You just want me to be a daddy to your kids."

"Why would you say something like that? Calvin, are you serious? When I married you, I married you and I accepted Lacey. I understand that you come with a package. That package, however, does not include Kim. Why is she always ... At some point in our marriage, why does her name always have to come up?"

"It comes up because you bring it up, Savannah. It's

like you're threatened by her."

"Threatened? Oh, I don't think so. I have no need to be threatened by her."

"You just can't accept the fact that there is a woman out there with my child When you accepted Lacey, you also knew that she had a mother. You knew that I would have to communicate with her mother. So why does it upset you so? You knew what you were dealing with. So, I don't want to hear it anymore. I don't want to hear you complaining about Lacey's mom again. She's going to be in my life as long as we're raising our daughter."

"You're right," Savannah began to cry. "Lacey is you and Kim's daughter."

"Man, whatever. You know what I meant."

"No, I definitely understood you correctly."
Savannah turned and walked away, realizing that
having a blended family was harder than she had
expected. Was it true? Maybe she got herself into
something she thought she could handle, but maybe
her insecurities were causing her to push Calvin
away. She walked into the kitchen and saw the cup
of coffee sitting on the counter that Calvin had
made for her. Because she was so angry, she
decided not to drink any coffee. Instead, she
grabbed the coffee mug, walked over to the sink and
poured it out. Calvin was only a few steps behind
her and noticed exactly what she had done and he
became furious at how ungrateful Savannah was
being.

Coffee Love   *Marita Kinney*

A couple of days had gone by and Savannah noticed that Calvin had stopped making coffee for her altogether. For some reason, she realized that she had hurt his feelings to the core. Something just seemed off, not having coffee with him. Ever since they started dating, they always had coffee together, every single morning. He always catered to her, but suddenly that stopped. Savannah knew that she couldn't go another day without speaking to Calvin and she had to make things better, so she made him some coffee instead, as a peace offering. She walked the coffee into his office where he was working. "Good morning, Calvin," Savannah said as she held out a cup of coffee, extending her arm to give it to him.

"Good morning, Savannah." Calvin replied in a cold tone.

"I made you some coffee." Calvin looked up and was surprised that selfish Savannah had finally made him a cup of coffee. "Would you like some?"

"Nah, I'm good." She couldn't believe that he denied the coffee that she made. Her feelings were equally hurt.

Savannah sighed, "Okay, well, let me know if you need anything."

"Uh-huh," Calvin replied.

Savannah turned around and headed back to the kitchen to pour out the coffee that she had made, before she reached the kitchen, she heard Calvin walking behind her. "You know what? Yeah, I'll take that coffee. I really need it. I've been up since

five o'clock this morning working on this website
and I really need to get it done and I appreciate you
making coffee for me." Savannah smiled, ecstatic
that Calvin had changed his mind. So, she handed
him the coffee with a smile and leaned up and gave
him a kiss on the cheek. He said thank you with his
eyes as he turned around and walked towards the
office. Savannah wanted to make things right. She
followed him back into the office, shut the door and
locked it behind her.

"Did you just lock my door?"

"Absolutely, Mr. Calvin. I did." He smiled,
knowing that Savannah wanted to make love to
him, to make up with him and to make things better.
She began to unbutton his shirt and began to kiss all
over his chest.

Coffee Love   *Marita Kinney*

Calvin set his coffee down and said, "I guess you're
going to give me some rich coffee this morning."

"That's right. I'm going to give you another type of
coffee." They began to make love on his desk,
pushing papers out of the way and connecting once
more, realizing that everything they had been
arguing about was foolish and Savannah was
turning over a new leaf.

Chapter 5
Make Up

Savannah made it up in her mind, what type of wife she wanted to become. Although it was her third marriage, she felt like a complete failure and felt lost as if she didn't know what she was doing. Calvin was special type of man. He was an alpha male. Although he was loving and charming, she knew that he would only take so much of her spoiled behavior before enough was enough. So, every morning, she made it a point to wake up, make love to him, get up and for once serve him, make him some coffee. Calvin was loving it. He didn't know where the change came from or how it happened, but he wasn't complaining about it. It had been several weeks since Savannah even mentioned Kim's name. He had fallen in love with her all over again and they were on top of the world. Nothing could come between them. Their marriage was getting stronger and he asked Savannah what had happened.

Savannah smiled as she was grateful that he finally asked where the change came from. "You know, Calvin. I was wondering when you were going to ask. I didn't tell you, but I've been going to counseling. The counseling had been really helping me see myself in another perspective and honestly, I didn't like what I seen, so I started to do some self-development and started reading more books and I just started working on me. At first, I thought I needed to work on our marriage, but then I realized that I couldn't work on our marriage until I dealt with me first and there were some changes that I needed to make for me and I'm proud to say that because of those changes, I am becoming a better wife for you."

Calvin reached over and gave Savannah a passionate kiss. "You know why I married you don't you?"

"Um, I'm guessing because you love me, right?" Wondering why Calvin said that.

"I married you because you're a strong woman. I married you because you have been hurt so much but I knew you had so much to give and with the help of God, I knew that things would turn around for us. You see, hurt people hurt other people and the only reason why you were lashing out and hurting me is because you were still hurting. I've been praying that God would continue to show you who you are so that you can see the woman that I see." Savannah began to cry as Calvin continued to pour his heart out to her. "See Savannah, you're a beautiful woman and there's no need for you to be angry. There's no need for you to be jealous or insecure. You're the best woman that I've ever known and there were some things that I needed to do also in order to make our marriage stronger. Setting boundaries with Kim was one of them and because of you, I was able to do that. All these years, I've been so afraid that she wouldn't allow me to see Lacey if I didn't, you know, dance to her drum, but you made me realize that I'm a father regardless and I didn't have to play by her rules. My job was to be a good father to Lacey, nothing more, nothing less."

Hearing those words from Calvin made Savannah feel good. She knew they were going in the right direction and knew that with God, they could get through anything.

Chapter 6
Girl Talk

Savannah's face lit up as she saw the phone. It was Ashton, her pretend little sister, a young lady that had had mentored for years, that now lived in Illinois with her new husband. She hadn't seen her in years, but they talked often, but because of the issues that they were going through in their marriage, she hadn't talked to Savannah in a couple of months and was excited to share how everything was going with her. "Hello?"

"Hey Savannah! How are you girl?"

"I'm good. I'm good. I was so happy you called me. I've been trying to call you for the longest, but I kept getting busy and I kept forgetting and then, you know, busy with the kids."

"Girl, I understand. You don't have to explain anything to me. How are the kids doing? And I can't wait to meet Lacey."

"Oh, my goodness, they are so beautiful. They actually look alike. It's so funny because when we are out, everybody assumes that Lacey's my daughter. You know, they always tell me how much she looks like me. I even made up a birth story, girl. People ask me about the kids all the time and I tell them that Lacey was the baby who weighed the most and how much stretch marks I got with her, and I just start laughing."

"Girl, you are so crazy. Oh, my goodness. You guys are such a cute family. I see all your pictures on

Facebook. I just wish I could come visit, but you know, with this work schedule, it's kind of crazy, but I promise I will be there to visit you soon and I can't wait to see the new house."

"Oh my God, girl, it's beautiful. Calvin has really, really looked out for us. I mean, his desire was to put us in a beautiful home and he did just that."

"Well, I will say, Calvin is a good man and you're a very, very blessed woman to have him. You deserve the best. You've been through a lot." Ashton said as she looked around the homeless shelter that she was currently living in.

Savannah sighed, "Yeah I know. But unfortunately, being married to me hasn't been easy. It's like I've been through so much, I was damaged goods."

Ashton paused, confused why Savannah would say something like that. "What do you mean? Damaged goods?"

"Ashton, you have no idea. I've been getting counsel because, I'm halfway crazy." Savannah began to laugh. "I have been through so much in relationships and so many bad are things happening over and over again, I stop living and was surviving. I had started pushing Calvin away too. I was becoming jealous of Lacey's mom, just not liking the fact that they co-parent when, in reality, I wish that I could co-parent, you know? But things are what they are and I just had to learn how to support his co-parenting versus being intimidated by it."

"Wow, Savannah. I mean, that's really mature of

you to be able to recognize that and do something about it." Ashton was surprised that Savannah was being so vulnerable with her. Normally Savannah remained extremely private.

"My counselor has really been helping me and I'm becoming a better wife. I wish I had his mom to talk to though. I try to focus on what we have in common and not what divides us. Calvin and I have this thing with coffee. I know it sounds really, really weird, but we both have a strong love for coffee."

Ashton started laughing. "Coffee? What do you mean?"

"I know it's really weird but we have this thing with coffee. We drink coffee together every single morning. It used to be him making me coffee all the time but now I make coffee for him. Then it turned into whoever was up first makes the coffee. You know, it's just this amazing thing. I actually look forward to drinking coffee with him every single day. I had no idea that coffee would have such a significant purpose in my marriage. When we we're arguing at one point, he stopped making coffee for me and that's how I started making coffee for him and now, even if we're upset with each other, we have like this unspoken rule. We still make each other coffee, reminding us of our love, our commitment to each other."

Savannah replied, "That is amazing. Who would have thought that coffee would hold your marriage together?"

Savannah nodded in agreement. "I know. It's like

God put coffee in our life to save our marriage."

"You keep saying, 'save your marriage.' Were things really that bad?"

"Oh yeah. Things were that bad. I mean, emotionally, I was just going through a lot. I eventually started to see a therapist and I realize that I was depressed. I had been depressed for years, but now I'm on the right track and I'm able to love Calvin the way that he needs to be loved."

"Well, Savannah, I'm so proud of you and I'm cheering for you guys. Calvin is a really good guy and I pray that you guys continue to make it work."

They continued their conversation for hours and Savannah was extremely grateful to have a real friend that understood her.

Chapter 7
Father-Daughter Dance

The Lacey was excited to be at the mall picking out her pretty dress to go to the father-daughter dance. Lacey wanted a red dress with sparkles. She insisted on this particular red dress.

"Lacey, I think you need a ... Let me see what size you're wearing now." She looked inside of Lacey's shirt at her tag to verify the dress size. "Yep, you probably wear a seven or eight, so get this one." She pulled the dress off of the rack, giving Lacey her appropriate size.

She walked over the dressing room and allowed waited on her to try on the dresses. Lacey came out twirling, Savannah laughed. The sales associate saw her and complimented her dress. "Oh, my goodness, you are so blessed. Look at those beautiful kids. You don't have twins, do you? I know this one's not a twin because she's too tall. Are they triplets or are they twins?"

Savannah laughed as the lady tried to figure out their ages. "No, actually they're all just stair-step, six, seven, and eight."

"Oh. Oh, awesome, awesome, awesome. Well, okay."

"Actually, I am about to be eight," Lacey said.

"I'm sorry. She's about to be eight, like in two days so ..."

"Oh, I get it. Yes, you definitely don't want to mess that up," the sales lady said. "Well, you all have a good day. Beautiful family."

"Thank you. Thank you so much," Savannah was glowing, proud of her beautiful kids. "Alright Lacey, go ahead and change back into your clothes so we can get home. The father-daughter dance is tonight." She rushed back to the dressing rooms to put her clothes back. The boys were restless so Savannah looked in her purse to offer them some candy. As Savannah was going through her purse, she remembered that she placed the bills in her there too. She began to open up the envelopes, trying to see what bills still needed to be paid, she then came across an insurance bill for Calvin.

She opened it up without any hesitation, knowing

that whatever bill he had, she needed to add it on her bill list to pay, but was surprised when she saw that it was his life insurance policy premium that was due and it listed Lacey as the beneficiary. Blood began to boil as she was so upset that he could still have Lacey listed as his beneficiary and not her, his wife. Her whole mood changed. Lacey was finished changing and the kids were now ready to go get something to eat from the food court. Savannah, with an attitude, declined. Instead, she decided to rush home to confront Calvin about the papers that she had found.

The whole way home, all she could think about was if Calvin was truly invested in their marriage, or was he just on a ride, hoping that things would turn out great. She pulled up to the driveway, could barely get out the car. She stormed into the house, leaving the kids outside to let themselves out of the car, walked in and saw Calvin sitting on the couch and gave him the premium papers.

Calvin looked at the papers and said, "What's this?"

"What's that? That's your insurance papers and I want to know why Lacey's listed as your beneficiary. I mean, she's only eight years old."

"Honey, I just haven't had a chance to change my beneficiary paperwork."

"Really? Really? We've been married going on a year and you haven't had time to change it? You told me you didn't have any life insurance. So, what is this? You just got this policy apparently. I'm looking at it and this is the first time I've ever seen this bill so either you were hiding it or you just got it."

Calvin knew that he was in way over his head. There was no way to convince Savannah that he had forgotten to change the policy when indeed, he had just started the policy.

"Calvin, I would just like to know. What was the purpose of doing this?"

"I just wanted to make sure that if something happened to me, the kids would be taken care of."

"The kids? I don't see Luke or Lacey's name on here. All I see is Lacey's name. I look at these kids like they're all mine and you're still separating them."

66

Calvin was upset at Savannah accusing him of playing favoritism.

"Why would you get a policy just for Lacey? I don't understand. Oh, you know, matter of fact, I do understand. It is what I thought it was. You don't plan on staying in this marriage, do you?"

Calvin didn't know what to say. He had gotten the policy to make sure that Lacey was always taken care of. In fact, he didn't list Savannah, Luke or Lacey anywhere on the policy. "Look Savannah, I was going to get another policy for you and the other kids."

"But why are you separating anything? Why do the kids have to be on anything? You should list me, as your wife. If something were to happen to you, I'm

going to make sure these kids are taken care of. You
don't trust me. That's what it boils down to. You
don't trust me to take care of Lacey if something
happens to you."

Instead of arguing, Calvin got up and began to walk
away. "Look Savannah, I'm the man of this house.
You're not going to keep questioning me. You
question my loyalty. You question everything that I
do as if I don't know how to take care of this family.
The reality is, I'm going to take care of Luke and
Lacey, but I also have an obligation to Lacey and I
have to make sure that if something happens to me,
Lacey's looked after as well. You may not like it,
but it is what it is. I'm also getting another policy
for you and the kids."

Savannah heard the anger in his voice and had

never heard him so upset so she shut up and stopped
picking an argument with him. Instead, she
retreated. She withdrew herself from the
conversation and just like a turtle, her head went
into a shell. She looked back and saw the kids
standing there with their bags as they were afraid to
say anything as they had just walked into a heated
argument. "Kids go upstairs, Lacey please take your
dress upstairs and put it away until it's time to get
dressed," Savannah said softly.

"Yes ma'am," said Lacey, old enough to understand
that whatever the argument was, it was about her
being treated differently than the other kids.

Chapter 8
Just Coffee

The father-daughter dance came and went; Calvin and Savannah still were not speaking to each other. Instead, they were going on with their daily routine: Getting up, getting dressed for work, putting the kids on the bus, coming home, eating dinner together, going to bed angry and waking up, doing it all over again. The one thing that was missing was them talking. They still weren't talking at all. They would just wake up and one of them would make the other a cup of coffee, depending on who would get up first. There was no thank you, there was no conversation, there were just mornings with silence and you could only hear the coffee brewing.

Coffee Love   *Marita Kinney*

It was as if they had gotten into this routine of misery together. Their marriage consisted of arguing, making up, arguing, making up and in between all of those was drinking coffee every day.

Coffee was the one thing holding them together.

Chapter 9
Divorce

It was 5:30 a.m. and Savannah heard Calvin

downstairs, moving about in the kitchen. She heard

the coffee pot brewing and knew that Calvin was

probably trying to make up with her. A smile was

upon her face as she got out of the bed, put on her

bathrobe and slid her feet in her slippers. She made

her way downstairs, anticipating having a cup of

coffee with her husband which she missed so much.

It wasn't the same when they weren't talking to

each other. She walked in the kitchen and noticed

Calvin already drinking his coffee, but to her

surprise, there wasn't another cup. Instead of saying

anything about it, she said nothing. She just began

to make her own cup of coffee as Calvin pretended

not to see her. This was more tension than she could handle.

After she made her cup of coffee, she sat down at the breakfast table and noticed a file folder laying there with her name on it. She opened it up and to her surprise; there was a petition for divorce. She tried to hold back the tears, but they flew down her face, soaking her bath robe as Calvin stood there and watched and said nothing. She slammed down her coffee mug, "Calvin, what's this?"

He said nothing and continued to sip his coffee.

"So, you want a divorce from me? All because what? Because I had questions about an insurance policy?"

Calvin became angry, flared his nostrils and replied
to Savannah in a very gentle tone, "You just don't
get it do you? This has nothing to do with an
insurance policy. This has everything to do with
you and the way you treat me. I don't deserve this
and if you're unhappy with me, you don't either. So
why don't we just stop pretending? I can't live the
rest of my life like this. Neither should you want to,
so divorce is the only solution. You can move on
with your life, Savannah. I'm not holding you
hostage and I can move on with mine."

Savannah sat, speechless. She couldn't believe what
she was hearing. Calvin wasn't only making a
threat. He was certain of his decision. Savannah
closed the file folder, and did not reply to Calvin.
She just swallowed her pride, stood up with her cup
of coffee and said, "If this is what you want, I'll give

you the divorce," as her voiced trembled with truth. The reality of her situation was unbearable. She began to breathe heavily as if she was having a panic attack. '

Calvin was irritated by her response and rolled his eyes. "Okay, so I guess you're going to play the victim now, right?"

She ignored him as she tried to pick up the pieces to her broken heart. "How could this happen," she thought to herself. "How could I not have known it was this bad?" She pleaded to understand how things had gotten so bad. She thought that divorce would only come if they just couldn't see eye-to-eye, if they were in an abusive relationship, if they were having financial difficulties. Whatever it was, she was going to weather the storm, but she never

thought about Calvin leaving her. She made a
commitment to be by his side. *Should I just give up
or should I fight for my marriage?* Too confused to
think of any solution, she went to her room, laid
back in the bed and began to cry, asking God to
reveal to her what had happened, asking God to
give her another chance. She knew she had blown
it, but would Calvin allow her close to her heart
again was the question she began to ponder on. No
matter what he had decided, she had to find peace
with her decisions and pushing him away is what
she had done.

She laid in bed as long as she could until she
couldn't take it anymore. She forced herself to get
dressed, do her hair. As she brushed it over and over
again, but it was difficult because her hair had
matted from all the tears that she had cried as she

laid on her pillow in distress. She was determined to look normal before she left the house. She didn't want anyone to know what she was going through, but she knew the one person that could help her was Lady Rose, but she had to be totally transparent with her as she often shifted the blame onto Calvin during her therapy sessions. She knew that she needed some spiritual guidance, but she had to admit that she had caused a lot of the damage.

She went to the church hoping to find someone to talk to, but she couldn't find anyone. In fact, no one was there. The church was closed. *Why is it that out of all days that she needed to talk to someone, no one was to be found?* She laughed to herself. "I guess you're trying to get my attention, God. I guess you want me to talk to you." She went to a park nearby that overlooked the pond. As she walked

down to the pier, she saw the ducks swimming.
They came closer to her but soon swam away as
they noticed she didn't have any bread to feed them.
Her eyes were swollen, nearly almost shut. She
cried until she had no more tears to cry. How could
she become so self-destructive? How could her
marriage be so bad? How could Calvin want a
divorce? Things weren't as bad as other couples. I
guess everybody had their breaking point and he
didn't want to live a life of misery. Instead of her
running, it was him.

Without anything else to do, she looked up and
began to pray to God. "God, I need you to help me
through this. I need you to help me because all I do
is turn all my relationships toxic and I'm so hurt and
I'm so broken. How can I reject the man who loved
me? How did I reject him? How did I not see the

signs that he needed me to be loving and kind and confident? Instead, I was secure. Instead, I was broken. Instead, I pretended to be so independent that I didn't need a man. I didn't need him to help me with the kids. I didn't let him discipline the kids. I pushed him away and Lord I'm sorry. Please soften his heart. God, please show me what to do. I don't know what I'm doing. I need You, Lord. I need You to step into my marriage. Lord, I'm handing this marriage over to You and I pray in the name of Jesus, God, that You bless this marriage and that you turn our hearts towards each other again. In Jesus' name, Amen."

Savannah sat for a few more hours, just watching the ducks, trying to figure out her life, trying to forgive herself, trying to accept that Calvin no longer wanted to be with her.

Coffee Love   *Marita Kinney*

Savannah was at work on her lunch break sitting in her car, listening to some gospel music and reading the Bible when she realized that it was her anniversary. It had been a couple weeks since she heard from Calvin since he had moved out. She was grateful that he was still paying the bills, but her beautiful house didn't seem like a home without him there. She no longer was seeing Lacey either, Kim refused to allow her to come see Savannah and the kids. Everything was just falling apart, but Savannah found the peace that she needed through the word of God. She believed that if it was meant for her marriage to work, God would change things around and although Calvin wasn't very kind to her, she still greeted him with a smile and kept things cordial.

When she would see him at church in passing, she pretended that she wasn't bothered by his cold shoulder. Nobody seemed to know that they were separated because Savannah was now singing in the choir and was so busy with church activities that she barely saw Calvin at church other than him preaching. She wanted to keep everything positive. She didn't want to wear her weariness on her face. Calvin was putting on a good show, the church would be in disbelief if they really knew the truth.

Savannah looked down at her ring that she was still wearing, she began to cry. She sent Calvin a friendly text message.

"I know this may seem crazy, but happy anniversary to us." She waited for a couple of minutes, but he didn't reply. She was hurt and she was broken. The marriage was really ending. They were getting a divorce and it seemed as if Calvin had lost every feeling of romance for her. She wasn't sure if the members of the church knew anything, but it was strange that no one mentioned their anniversary in latest announcements.

Every attempt that she made to reach out to Calvin, he ignored her, but still, Savannah was his wife and she was going to do whatever she could to get him back. She said she wasn't going to fight the divorce, but something inside of her wouldn't let her throw it away. She was still in love with him. Throwing her marriage away was not an option. The devil could not have it.

Chapter 10

Savannah began to think of things in a matter of serving her husband, instead of only looking at what he could do for her. She knew that he was in a hotel and that he could only get coffee in the lobby, so she wanted to surprise him. While he was at work, she delivered a Keurig Coffee Maker to the front desk with some coffee and his favorite creamer, along with a, "I'm thinking of you," card. Inside she wrote,

"Dear Calvin,

I know how much you love your morning coffee so I wanted you to have this. So, every morning you could wake up and make your favorite coffee. I love you.

Your wife,

Savannah."

She sealed the card and handed it to the receptionist. "Can you please deliver this to Calvin Snow's room?"

"Sure, I'll have housekeeping put it inside."

"Great," Savannah smiled as she walked away. She felt good about serving. Why didn't she think of this earlier? Why didn't she give more? Why was she just taking, taking, taking? Nevertheless, things were changing and at least she felt good about knowing that she was doing the best she could to win Calvin's heart again.

It was 6:00 p.m. in the evening and Savannah had just finished dinner for the kids when she got a phone call. She grabbed her cell phone and was surprised it was Calvin. She answered the phone with hesitation, not knowing what he was going to say.

"Hello, this is Savannah."

"Hey Savannah. How are you doing?"

"I'm good. It's good to hear your voice."

"I just wanted to say thank you for the Keurig. That was really thoughtful of you."

"Oh, no problem. I knew it was probably painful for you to have to go the lobby every day to make

Coffee Love   *Marita Kinney*

coffee and I wanted you to feel like you had a piece
of home with you."

Calvin smiled on the other end of the phone. "I
really appreciate that and also I wanted to know if,
um, if you would like to meet me for
some…Well… Maybe we can … You know, maybe
we can go somewhere and have a cup of coffee
together. I mean, after all, we don't have to be
enemies."

Savannah laughed, "Enemies. Never that. I mean,
you're my husband."

Calvin got quiet as he thought of Savannah just
calling him her husband although they were in the
middle of a divorce, she still called him her
husband. It made him feel good. "Look, um, maybe

tomorrow before you go into work, you could meet me at our favorite uh ... At our favorite restaurant."

"Oh, okay. Cool. Well, I'll see you. I'll see you in the morning. I love you," Savannah said boldly and awaited a reply.

Calvin hesitated, but before he hung up, he replied, "I love you too," as he hung up the phone.

Conclusion

This story is to symbolize a lot of things that married people go through. Although some of you may not have been through exactly what this couple went through. Maybe you've gone through more. Maybe you feel like you have the perfect marriage and haven't gone through anything. But I encourage you to find that one thing that's going to hold you together. In this story it was coffee. It may seem far-fetched, but there are so many levels of truth in it. Although the things that happened in this story did not happen to me, I wanted to share this story because coffee is one thing that I look forward to drinking with my husband every morning. We wake up and we have coffee together. We've done it for

years. I was inspired by my own marriage and the
love that my husband and I have for coffee and each
other. I wanted to share it with you, to inspire you
to stay connect anyway that you can. It could be
something so little in the toughest times that can
hold you together.

In fact, I remember moving to a small town and
they didn't have a café, so my husband and I bought
a building and we started our own café. You know,
coffee is one of those things that comforts people.
They feel like they have to have it in the morning,
but one of the things that makes it even better, is
having someone to share it with. I enjoy drinking
coffee with my husband and through this story, I
pray, that those of you that are married can review
your own life and see what it is that you and your
husband do together that makes a particular thing so

special. Find it and hold onto it, because in the

tough times, that might be the one thing that will

save your marriage. God bless.

If you enjoyed this book, try following the entire series.

The Snow Series, Broken Family

Snow's Meltdown

Description: What happens when everything around you may seem perfect - your family, your health, your social status, your overall life - but all of a sudden something threatens to tear it all apart and rob you of what you've always known? This type of thing happens to many people, every day, from all walks of life. Some are able to get over it and go on with their lives. But others are not so fortunate. They find themselves stuck in their own meltdown of loss, hurt, and pain. Such is the situation in Marita L. Kinney's latest novel.

Don't Rescue Me, God's Molding Me

Description: Savannah is a sophisticated single mother who has had her share of growing pains. From rags to riches, back to rags, Savannah is determined to change her circumstance through her faith and perseverance. As she struggles to keep her head above water, her new vindictive neighbors, try her patience and her faith. She desperately desires for God to rescue her from her new life of struggle.

Seed Of Discord

Description: The Snow family continues to push through their issues, until Pastor Snow takes a special interest in a prostitute named Candy. His wife, Lady Snow is dying of cancer and that doesn't seem to make him cut ties with Candy, although his reputation is on the line. Will the family have another meltdown or will they persevere? A Christian Fiction Novella that offers healing, deliverance, and restoration.

Coffee Love

Description: Calvin and Savannah were the perfect couple, until they began to have issues with their blended family. Savannah struggles with insecurities which pushes Calvin away and he's ready to end the marriage. Their family has been through a lot, but is he willing to throw everything away to end the stress.

Looking for Love in All the Wrong Places

Description: Grace could get any man she wanted physically, but obtaining love seemed to be impossible for her. Although she appeared to be very strong, independent, and very charming, she was empty on the inside. Grace had a great career and achieved many accomplishments. However, when it came to her love life, she felt like a complete failure. Until she decided to no longer be held captive to sexual abuse in the past.

Pastor Calvin Snow

Description: Calvin Snow is the new Associate Pastor of Mount Zion and the attention from the single ladies is becoming irresistible. Although his wife Savannah tries to keep things spicy in the bedroom, Calvin finds his life boring and predictable. The couple struggles to stay connected in the midst of all the adversity.

Temptation

Description: Calvin Snow is the new Associate Pastor of Mount Zion and the attention from the single ladies is becoming irresistible. Although his wife Savannah tries to keep things spicy in the bedroom, Calvin finds his life boring and predictable. The couple struggles to stay connected in the midst of all the adversity.

About Author

Dr. Marita L Kinney is a publisher, metaphysical practitioner, and entrepreneur. She has inspired thousands of people to overcome adversity with triumph through faith and perseverance. While facing several life-changing challenges herself, Dr. Kinney had enough faith to conquer tribulations, coming out victorious. Capturing the true essence of what it means to turn "lemons into lemonade," she has taken the harsh lessons of life and developed a plan for successfully living.

As an Inspirational Publishing Expert and entrepreneur, she has coached thousands of people, helping them to become published authors, build a platform, and create passive income through entrepreneurship. To date, she has taught nearly 8,000 students in over 139 countries, has written and published over 58 titles and through her publishing company, Pure Thoughts Publishing, LLC, has helped authors all over the world share their stories and expertise. Her business coaching skills allow her clients to easily obtain the necessary steps to move their book, business, and life forward.

Dr. Kinney's clients learn how to weave their inspired ideas into actionable steps that are applied to their daily life, regardless of where they are or what obstacles they must overcome to achieve their desired results. She has been featured on *The Steve Harvey Show*, business magazines such as *Black Enterprise*, and countless interviews.

www.ingramcontent.com/pod-product-compliance
Lightning Source LLC
Chambersburg PA
CBHW052014240626
47153CB00008B/2866